Never Catch a Cold

André François

Never Catch a Cold

Long ago, the world was full of strange creatures.
I'm not sure what this one was. It had no name.

The Cube
had no wings,
no hands,
no legs, and
no tail. It had
no practical
use, so it has
vanished.

here is a six-foot-tall man looking at a Cube at the Museum of Natural History

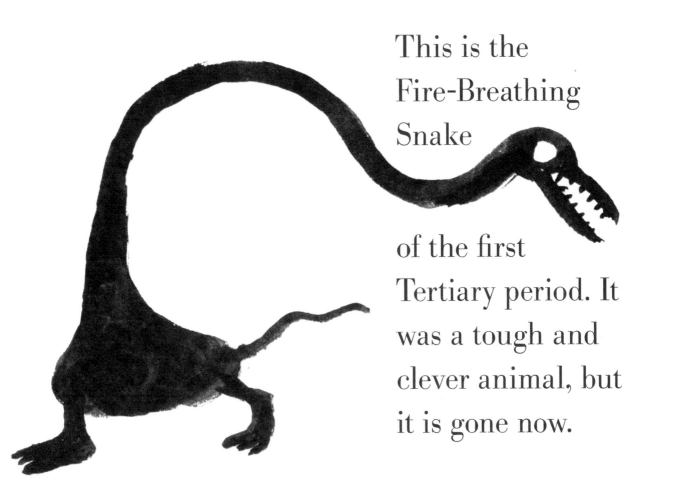

This is the Fire-Breathing Snake

of the first Tertiary period. It was a tough and clever animal, but it is gone now.

No one knows for certain that the Strumpf even existed. It seems to have been eliminated by the automobile era.

here is a headless Strumpf

The Dogter
might have made
a friendly pet
had it survived
to modern
times.

The Jam-Eating
Frog has likewise
disappeared.

Two others worth mentioning

are the Mammoth and the Drawer-Eagle.

But...

The *C*old survived
them all. Why?

Because, from the time
we are little children,
we are taught to
never catch a *Cold*.

The very first *C*olds originated
in prehistoric Ice-Coldland.

All *C*olds are equal, just like you and I.

But there are many varieties of *C*olds.

The Common *C*old.

The Head Cold.

The Hay Fever Cold.

The Traveling Cold.

The Serious Cold.

The Treated Cold.

The Neglected Cold.

The Imminent
*C*old.

The Big Bad *C*old.

The Sniffles Cold.

You still have to go to school.

The Violent *C*old.

(Sometimes called the Rifle *C*old.)

Colds can be divided

into two classes:

Good Colds and Bad Colds.

My mom had a Gentle *C*old that wouldn't go away.

But Grandpa was done in by a Mean Cold.

Everyone knows the cough.
It is a parasite of the Cold.

Some people stay in bed for days

if they catch a *C*old.

Colds can be very complicated.

It is not easy to get rid of a Cold.

Some say you should never take a bath
with a *C*old.

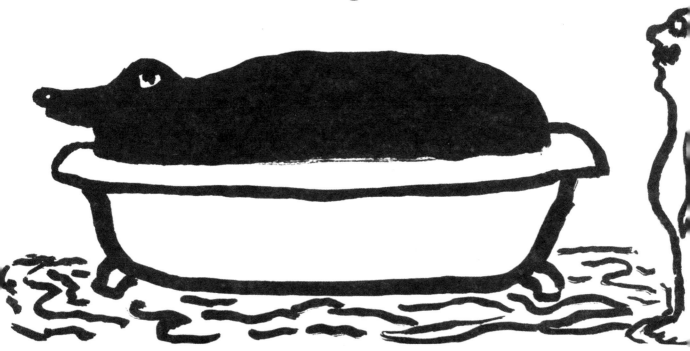

In this big world, there are shoals of herring.

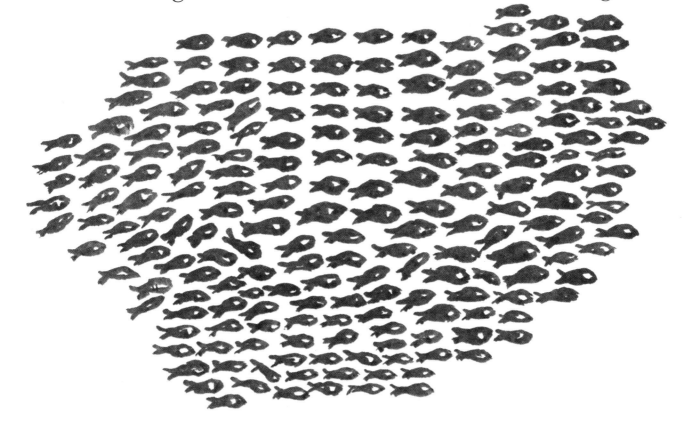

Flocks of sheep.

Schools of turbot.

And

epidemics

of Colds.

You can catch a Cold easily.

But given the choice,
the wise person tries not to.

Which is why …

There are always …

Way too many …

Colds.

André *François* (1915–2005) was an influential, Romanian-born French artist. He painted, sculpted, designed posters and theater stages, and worked in graphic design but became best known for his work as a cartoonist. His illustrations—defined by their humor, satire, and surreal, often black-and-white style—have been published around the world in magazines such as *The New Yorker*. He also created many books, including the cartoon anthology *The Penguin André François* and the acclaimed children's book *Crocodile Tears*.

André François Les Rhumes © 2011 Delpire Editeur, Paris
Illustrations and text copyright © André François
This edition © 2012 The Creative Company, under license from Delpire Editeur, Paris
All rights for publishing in other languages and/or other reproduction
of illustrations reserved to Delpire Editeur, Paris.
Adapted from the original work made for the Laboratoires Beaufour advertising campaign in 1966.
Translation adapted by Aaron Frisch Design adapted by Rita Marshall
Creative Editions is an imprint of The Creative Company www.thecreativecompany.us
P.O. Box 227, Mankato, MN 56002 USA
Printed in Shenzhen, China   0412 RRD 12000974
Library of Congress Cataloging-in-Publication Data
François, André, 1915–2005. [Rhumes. English]
Never catch a cold / written and illustrated by André François. Summary: Black ink illustrations
help introduce various kinds of colds—and a number of fantastical creatures that are now extinct—
in this humorous narrative about the history of our most common illness.
ISBN 978-1-56846-231-8
1. French wit and humor, Pictorial. 2. Cold (Disease)—Juvenile literature. I. Title.
NC1499.F72A4 2012   741.5'6944–dc23   2012000045
First edition
2 4 6 8 9 7 5 3 1